W9-DID-100

Copyright © 2001 by Michael Neugebauer Verlag, Nord-Süd Verlag AG,
Gossau Zürich, Switzerland
First published in Switzerland under the title *Der Apfelkönig*
English translation copyright © 2001 by North-South Books, Inc.
All rights reserved. No part of this book may be reproduced or utilized in
any form or by any means, electronic or mechanical, including photocopying,
recording, or any information storage and retrieval system, without
permission in writing from the publisher.
First published in the United States, Great Britain, Canada,
Australia, and New Zealand in 2001 by North-South Books,
an imprint of Nord-Süd Verlag AG, Gossau Zürich, Switzerland
Distributed in the United States by North-South Books, Inc., New York
Library of Congress Cataloging-in-Publication Data is available
A CIP catalogue record for this book is available from The British Library
ISBN 0-7358-1397-3 (trade) 10 9 8 7 6 5 4 3 2 1
ISBN 0-7358-1398-1 (library) 10 9 8 7 6 5 4 3 2 1
Printed in Germany
For more information about our books, and the authors and artists
who create them, visit our web site: www.northsouth.com

THE APPLE KING

By Francesca Bosca
Illustrated by Giuliano Ferri
Translated by J. Alison James

A Michael Neugebauer Book
North-South Books · New York · London

In a very old castle, surrounded by walls, lived a rich and powerful king. In the king's garden grew a magnificent apple tree, that bore the sweetest and most beautiful apples. The king was very proud of his apple tree.

Every day throughout the summer, the king went into the garden to watch the apples as they grew. In the autumn, the king himself climbed up a ladder to pick his apples. He washed them and polished them until they gleamed like jewels. Then he displayed them in the castle as if they were priceless ornaments.

No one but the king himself was permitted to touch the apples—and of course no one but the king was allowed to eat them!

The king's head gardener was assigned to do nothing else but care for the royal apple tree. He watered it, loosened the earth around the roots, and even dusted the bark clean with a little brush. But his most important job was to guard the tree and make certain that nobody came near it.

Despite all this, one morning the head gardener made a horrifying discovery: one of the apples had a deep and ugly hole.

The head gardener ran directly into the castle.
"Your Majesty," he cried, his voice trembling.
"In one of your Royal Apples, there
appears to be a worm!"
"WHAAAT???" The king roared so loudly
that he could be heard throughout
the entire castle. The poor head gardener
was immediately demoted to the lowest
weeder in the royal vegetable garden.

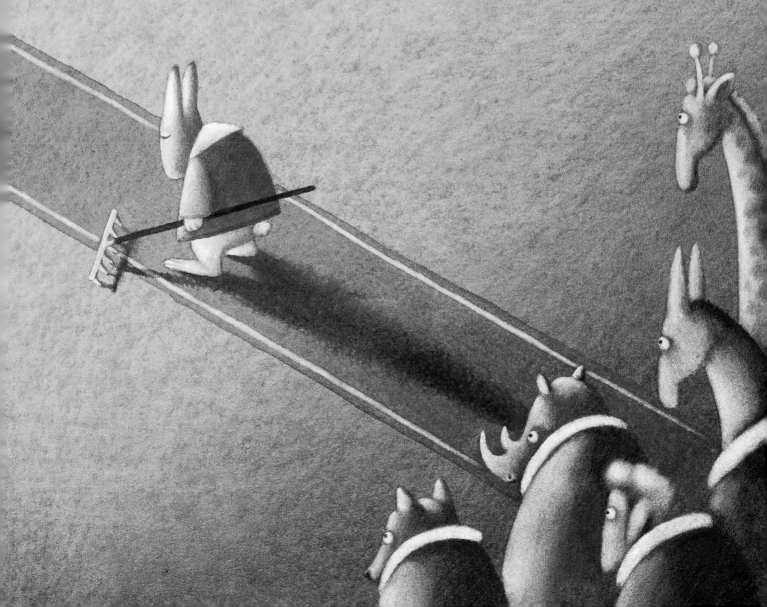

The king ran outside to observe the damage. It was terrible! There wasn't just one single worm—there were worms in every apple on the tree!

"My poor apples," whimpered the king. Then, remembering what worked so often in times of conflict, he flattered them and offered a bribe.

"Venerable worms, if you would be so kind as to depart from my apples, I will give you a sack full of gold!"

"Pish posh," scoffed the worms. "We can't eat gold." And they stayed where they were.

When the king saw that he couldn't solve the problem that way, he summoned the greatest and most powerful magicians in the kingdom. They scrutinized the apple tree from its roots to its crown, sprinkled it with magic potions, and murmured mysterious spells.

The worms disappeared, but by the next night they were back, hungrier than ever.

The king was furious. "Enough!" he roared. "I will show these fiends who is in charge here!" He marched the entire royal army up to the tree, and within minutes they had the worms surrounded.

"Kill them, kill them all!" commanded the king. "But woe on you if you injure a single apple or harm my precious tree!"

Now, this was quite impossible. Every worm was in an apple, and every apple was on the tree. The royal army was forced to make a humiliating retreat.

The worms laughed and kept munching away on the sweet apples.

The king was beside himself. He sent out a proclamation declaring a reward of a sack of gold to anyone who could make the worms disappear.

A sly fox had his assistant climb the tree and cover up all the worm holes with thick red paint. Then they called the king. "Finished," they said. "There is not a worm to be seen."

The king was overjoyed. The sly fox and his accomplice disappeared with the sack of gold, and the king climbed up the tree to pick some apples. His mouth was already watering as he rushed back to the castle with a bowl filled with the luscious fruit.

But no sooner had the king taken a bite from the first apple when a worm crawled out and climbed on his nose.

"NOOOO!" bellowed the king. "What right do you wretched worms have to invade *my* apples?"

"But . . . but . . . but . . . we were invited!" said one of the apple worms.

"Invited! *Who* could have invited *you*?" shrieked the king.

"Why, the Royal Apple Tree invited us," explained the worm. "You see, year after year she bears beautiful apples for nobody but you. No butterfly and no bird may visit her. No child may climb in her branches and take a sweet apple. The poor apple tree was terribly sad and lonely. Finally she invited us since we were small enough to sneak past the guard. At last she was happy that others could appreciate her fruit."

"What about *me*?" the king asked angrily. "I love my precious apple tree, and I adore my royal apples!"

"Do you think so?" asked the worm. "Are you sure you really care about what's best for the Royal Apple Tree?"

The king was hurt. How dare a worm speak to him this way? The entire royal household was staring at the worm in stunned surprise. But what came next shocked them all. The king laughed!

"She is a remarkable tree," he declared. "And I will show her how much we all appreciate her. Everyone here will go out now and pick her beautiful apples. And this evening we will hold a Royal Apple Festival, with Apple Cider and Royal Apple Cake for all!"

Hearing this, the worms gladly abandoned the apples and crept off to get ready for the Festival.

It was a most splendid Apple Festival!
The king had never felt more proud
than when everyone praised the
wonderful taste of his apples.
And the people were proud of
their king, whose generosity
was as sweet as his apples!

From that day forward, each year at harvest time, the Royal
Apple Festival was celebrated at the castle. The rich and
powerful king had discovered that the royal apples
tasted even more delicious when shared with
cheerful company. And if the occasional
apple worm was seen among
the guests, the king was
not bothered in the least.